This book belongs to

....

D1401706

Written by Rosie Greening.
Illustrated by Stuart Lynch.

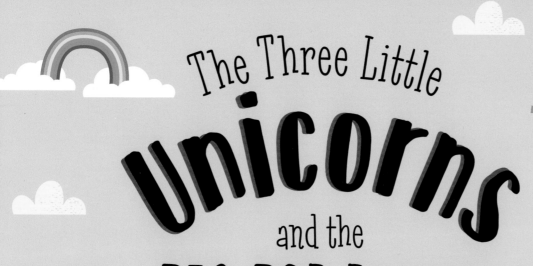

The Three Little Unicorns

and the
BIG, BAD Dragon

Rosie Greening • Stuart Lynch

make
believe
ideas

Cookie, Cloud, and Caramel were clever unicorns.

They made *delicious food* with their *amazing magic horns.*

Every day,
they *filled*
their house

with *toffee*,
cake,
and *treats*.

Their mom could *barely move*
for all the *snacks* around her *feet*.

Soon, their home was **CHOC-A-BLOCK**
with *yummy* food *galore.*

cookie

cloud

caramel

Caramel Sauce

The beds *brimmed*
with **BANANA BREAD**
and *cupcakes* filled the *floor!*

Mom said, "Little unicorns, there's no room now you've grown. You need to make your tasty treats in houses of your own."

Mom♥

Cakes

So *Cookie, Cloud,* and *Caramel*
packed up and **left** that day.

"Beware the *dragon —*
he's a **GRUMP!"**
they heard their mother say.

Cloud went off to Candy Land to build her *new house* there. It was made of **COTTEN CANDY,** so it looked as *light as air!*

Soon she heard a
giant
THUD
and then some
grouchy
roars:

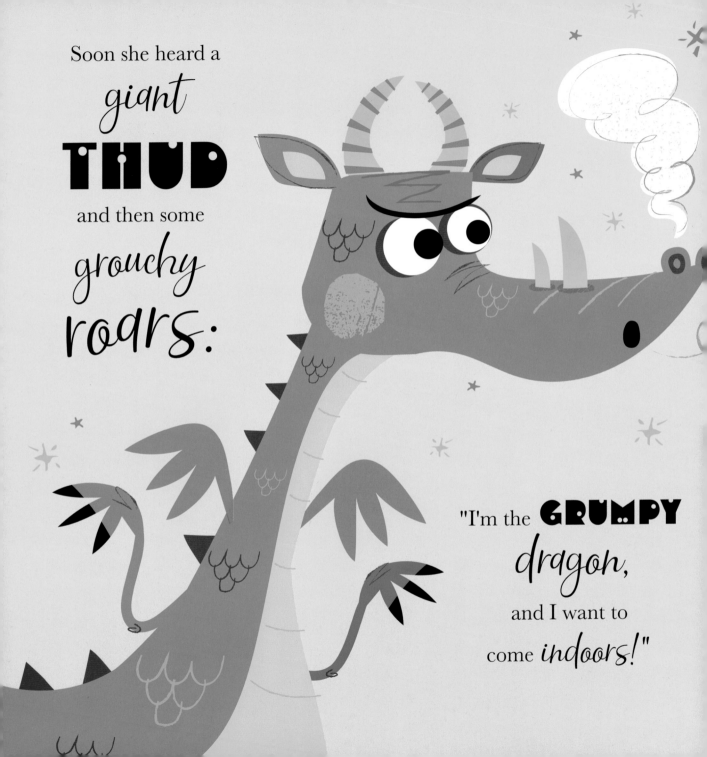

"I'm the **GRUMPY**
dragon,
and I want to
come *indoors!*"

Cloud thought he was very *rude* and said,

"You *can't*, so SHUSH!"

But the *dragon* HUFFED and *puffed* until . . .

. . . the house *flew* with a

whoosh!

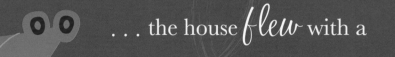

Cloud cried, "EEK!"
and cantered to the frosty *Land of Snow*,
where *Caramel* had built herself
an *ice-cream bungalow*.

Caramel gave Cloud a hug and said,
"You're safe in here.

This bungalow is frozen stiff:
the dragon won't get near!"

Soon, the *dragon* landed – **THUMP.**

"LET ME IN!" he *roared.*

"You're a *grump!*"
the pair replied.
"Prepare to be *ignored!*"

But *dragons* have a clever trick for *icy homes* like these.

He went **"AH-CHOO!"** to *melt* the house with one big, *fiery sneeze!*

The *house* was soon a **PUDDLE,**
so the pair *left* with a *trot.*

They had to get to *Rainbow Land* –
their sister's favorite **SPOT!**

Cookie's home was **GIANT-SIZED,**
and made of *gingerbread.*
It had a *rainbow* rock-cake roof with *turrets* overhead.

"You're *safe* in here," said *Cookie*,
when she heard her *sisters' tale.*

Chocolate

"Nothing gets through *gingerbread* —
the dragon's sure to *fail!"*

Soon enough,
the dragon *swooped*
and *landed* right
OUTSIDE.

"Now I'm even *grumpier*, so
LET ME IN!" he cried.

The unicorns *ignored* him,
so he **HUFFED** and *puffed* instead.

But *nothing* seemed to *budge*

the house of sturdy *gingerbread!*

"It's time for
Operation Sneeze,"
the dragon said.

"AH-CHOOOOOO

OOOOOOOOOOO!"

But all it did was make the *house*
smell extra *yummy*, too!

The *dragon* had one last idea
to make his way *inside*.

He flew up to the *chimney*,

and then—

whoosh—

began to

slide!

With a *splash*, he landed
in a *pool* of something **sweet.**

Chocolate

He *licked* the **CHOCOLATE**, *grinned*,
and said: "Could I have more to *eat?*"

He said, "I heard about your *treats!* I'm *sorry* I was *rude.*

Chocolate

I *always* get so **GRUMPY** when I'm *hungry* for some food."

"*Don't worry!*" said the *unicorns.*

"*We don't mind* in the least."

They *waved* their *horns*
and made him a
delicious, *dragon feast!*

At last, the little unicorns knew how to use their treats.

Café Open Today!

And the dragon was DELIGHTED now he had a place to eat!

The Three Little Unicorns
and the
BIG, BAD Dragon

When the three little *unicorns* fill their home with *treats*,
they move out and build *houses* of their own. There's just one problem:
the greedy **DRAGON** is around, and he's in a **GRUMPY** mood!
Will the *unicorns cheer up* the dragon, or will he blow their houses down?

Find out in this *magical twist* on the tale of
The Three Little Pigs, perfect to read together.

Written by Rosie Greening
Illustrated by Stuart Lynch

⚠ **WARNING:**
CHOKING HAZARD—Small parts.
Not for children under 3 yrs.

⚠ **ATTENTION :**
RISQUE DE SUFFOCATION—
Contient de petites pièces. Non recommandé
pour les enfants de moins de 3 ans.

make believe ideas

The Wilderness, Berkhamsted, Hertfordshire, HP4 2AZ, UK.
501 Nelson Place, P.O. Box 141000, Nashville, TN 37214-1000, USA.

Recommended for children aged 3 years and over.
Manufactured in China.

www.makebelieveideas.com

$4.99 U.S. $5.

ISBN10: 1-78947-867-7
ISBN13: 978-1-78947-867-9

50499

9 781789 478679

092020

"Well, of course you can come—the more the merrier!" replied SpongeBob.

"Oh, goody!" Plankton said, rubbing his little hands together. "I wouldn't miss it for the world."

The party was about to start.
Mr. Krabs was very excited.
"With so many payin' customers,
and, um, good friends, how could
anything ruin the night?"

Patrick hung the last of the garland as SpongeBob
decorated a batch of gingerkelp cookies. Everything
was perfect! Soon the guests started to arrive.

The party was a festive success! Everyone sang carols. Mr. Krabs gave SpongeBob a new spatula. SpongeBob gave Sandy a lasso. Then the doors swung open. Cold wind blew in.

A giant box tied with ropes stood in the doorway.
It seemed to roll into the restaurant by itself.
   Suddenly, a little figure jumped up onto the box.

"Ho, ho, ho!" Plankton exclaimed. "When I was looking through my telescope last night, I noticed your tree was missing something, so I wanted to give you a surprise you'd never forget!"

Plankton opened the box. Inside was a single golden star with a cord and a plug.

"This is no ordinary star," he said as he carried the ornament to the top of the tree and plugged it in. It was the brightest star anyone had ever seen.

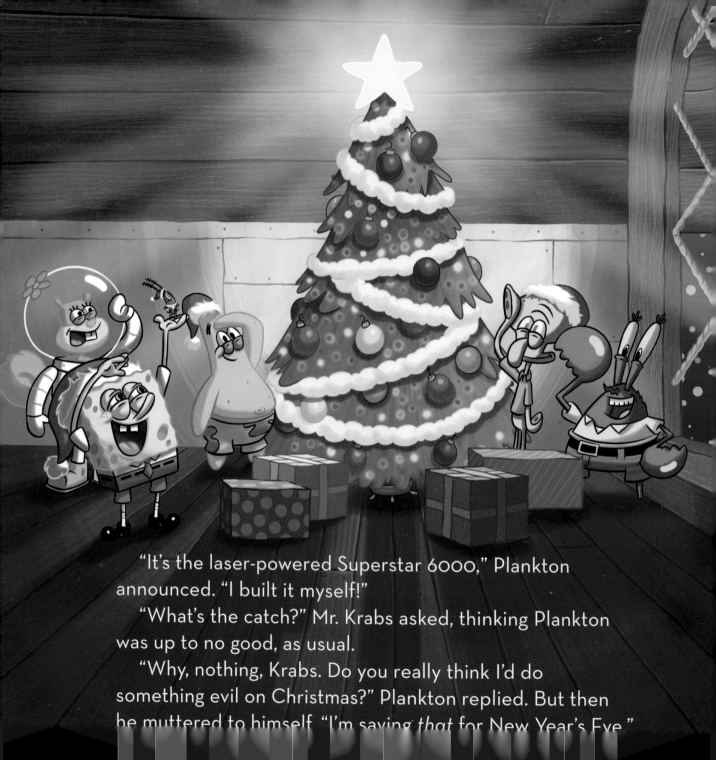

"It's the laser-powered Superstar 6000," Plankton announced. "I built it myself!"

"What's the catch?" Mr. Krabs asked, thinking Plankton was up to no good, as usual.

"Why, nothing, Krabs. Do you really think I'd do something evil on Christmas?" Plankton replied. But then he muttered to himself, "I'm saving *that* for New Year's Eve."